The Puppa-na-Wuppana Series

Living the Puppa-na-Life

by
Cindy Koebele and Lori Weaver

Illustrated by
Michael LaDuca

Koebele Weaver Enterprises, LLC
Mahtomedi, Minnesota

Copyright © 2016 by Koebele Weaver Enterprises, LLC

Koebele Weaver Enterprises, LLC
720 Arcwood Road
Mahtomedi, MN 55115
koebeleweaver.com

Book design and illustrations by Michael LaDuca, Luminus Media LLC

ISBN: 978-0-9909202-2-9

Library of Congress Control Number: 2015938126

Printed in the United States of America

Publisher's Cataloging-In-Publication Data
(Prepared by The Donohue Group, Inc.)

Koebele, Cindy.
  Living the Puppa-na-life / by Cindy Koebele and Lori Weaver ; illustrated by Michael LaDuca.

    pages : illustrations ; cm. -- (The Puppa-na-wuppana series ; [8])

    Summary: "My name is Puppa-na-wuppana and I am a Beagle dog. I have a special, magical nose. It helps me find things, but sometimes it gets me into trouble. Share my story as I get adopted and then learn all the new, fun places to explore and new friends to meet in my new home. A chapter book for early readers."
    Interest age level: 004-008.
    ISBN: 978-0-9909202-2-9

    1. Beagle (Dog breed)--Juvenile fiction. 2. Nose--Juvenile fiction. 3. Dog adoption--Juvenile fiction. 4. Beagle (Dog breed)--Fiction. 5. Nose--Fiction. 6. Dog adoption--Fiction. I. Weaver, Lori. II. LaDuca, Michael. III. Title.

PZ7.1.K64 Li 2016
[E]   2015938126

Table of Contents

Dedication

This book is dedicated to my two sons, Alec and André, who so badly wanted a puppy and brought love and inspiration to the concept of calling him Puppa-na-Wuppana. Also to my sister Angela who was the first person to tell me what a cute puppy wuppy our little beagle was.

- Cindy Koebele

Puppa-na-Love

Hello! My name is Puppa-na-Wuppana. Children say my name is a tongue twister, so sometimes I am called Puppa Wuppa, Puppa or just PW. My family says I am their dog, a Beagle dog to be exact. Hmmm, I wonder what a Beagle dog is. Is it how I look? Is it how I act? Or maybe how I talk? I am not sure, but what I do know is that I am very special and I lead a very special life.

When I was just eight weeks old I joined my new family. I hear they drove quite far in order to adopt me. When they peered into the pen that held me and my brothers and my sisters, our eyes locked, I wagged my tail, we smiled at each other and our fates were sealed. We became a family! While Mom drove the long way home, my two new brothers, Alec and André, cuddled me and kissed my nose the whole time! It was wonderful!

My new house was big!!! I was a little scared! I thought I might get lost. I was very careful to never let Mom, Alec, or André out of my sight…ever!

Bedtime came that first night and Mom put me inside a square box she called a kennel…in the laundry room…ALONE!! I was so sad and scared! I cried and scratched at the kennel door until Mom finally came to see me. She scooped

me up and gave me a little hug! I covered her face
in thankful kisses, thinking I was saved, but she
just kissed me once more and put me back into
that scary box saying, "Puppa, you need to go
night-night".

Wait! This would not do! I was lonely! I
cried and scratched and I waited for Mom to
come back. It had worked before, why not now?
But Mom did not come back even though I cried
and scratched all night long. I did not sleep at all.

The next night when bedtime came again, I
got very nervous. Did I have to go in that lonely
box again? My eyes pleaded with Mom, "Please
don't put me in that kennel box again".

Hurray! It worked. Mom placed me in a
big, soft warm bed with Alec and André. She told
the boys, "I didn't sleep well last night, because

Puppa-na-Wuppana was lonely and cried all night in his kennel. He is just a baby and needs to sleep with you boys"! I sighed with relief and snuggled deeper into the covers. That suited me perfectly. I guess when I didn't sleep all night neither did my family!

Puppa-na-Keekers

It was just Mom, Alec, André and me for the earlier years of my life. Oh, and Keekers! I must tell you all about her! She was black and furry and when she was really happy, a strange sound came out from her neck. It rumbled and sounded like "purrrrrrrr". We quickly became best friends. From the very moment our eyes first met and she batted my arm with her paw, we both knew it was love at first sight.

Having a playmate in the house was fantastic! We loved to run through the house playing and wrestling. Keekers showed me every nook and cranny of our house and I was no longer afraid of getting lost! Sometimes our play became a little too loud and a little too "rough and tumble", as Mom put it. She did not smile at this, especially when we knocked over lamps and plants. She would scold us and say, "Stop fighting like cats and dogs"! Keekers and I just looked at each other...huh? What does that mean? Then with a little shrug of our shoulders, we played even harder!

Hide and seek was our favorite game. Keekers could climb very high but I could not. This used to make me sad because I could not see her, but then, I discovered my nose was so powerful...sniff...sniff...sniff...I could SMELL her! This was how I discovered that I had a special nose, and not just special ...magical! Keekers soon found out that even though I might

not see her when she hides, she is no match for
my magical nose!   Found you, Keekers.
Victory is mine!

Puppa-na-Rule

When I lived with my Beagle mom and brothers and sisters, there were no rules.   We just played, ate and slept in one big pen. I could even do my "business" whenever and wherever I wanted.

I soon found out with my new family, in my new house, this was not allowed!! I was expected to do my "business" only outdoors and if that wasn't enough, I was also supposed to tell them WHEN I needed to go outdoors to do my "business"! That was very hard for me to remember!   After all, I might be playing or sleeping and forget about this whole "business" rule!

Sometimes I would remember this new "business" rule just a little too late and have an accident in the house. Mom was not happy at all with accidents. She would scold the boys for not paying attention to me and cried, "Puppa-na-Wuppana had an accident"! Then she would pick me up and put me outside and say, "No treat for you when you do your "business" in the house"! What?! I love treats! My magical nose smells treats from miles away! I vowed to try very hard to learn this "business" rule. Then I saw the boys' sad faces. Well, at least I wasn't the only one in trouble with Mom. When Mom wasn't happy, none of us were happy.

Puppa-na-Chewy

My family and I had a hard time during what Mom called the "teething" stage. I didn't know what that word meant...I just knew my teeth HURT! Puppy teeth are very sharp. The only thing that helped my teeth to feel better was to chew, chew and chew some more! Luckily, there were so many interesting choices to pick from in my house!

I got scolded quite a lot during this "teething" time. I guess the things I found to chew on were not always things that should be chewed on by puppies! Mom's expensive high

heels made my teeth feel so much better. It also made Mom cry when she found them, and that made me sad too, but I just couldn't resist them!

After several delicious pairs, she started to keep her closet door closed and I was forced to look for something new to chew on. Hmmm... furniture corners or the couch...I wonder if I would get scolded for that? I peeked into Alec and André's room. Maybe Alec's sunglasses or André's ski gloves might feel good on my teeth? In fact, their bedroom floor was covered in choices! One thing for sure, I could always count on Alec and André to come through for me with some "Puppa-na-Chewy".

Puppa-na-Santa

When I was about six months old a strange event happened in my house. My family brought in a large green tree and put sparkling lights and pretty hanging balls all over it. I was very curious about this as the only trees I had ever seen were outside and they certainly did not sparkle! Soon after, Mom started putting colorful boxes and bags underneath the branches of the tree. It was so new and exciting. What was inside those bags and boxes? Maybe a treat for me? Was there something for a Puppa-na-Wuppana? I could not wait to look inside them!

One night after we all went to bed, I woke up to stretch and noticed that someone had left the bedroom door open. Immediately I was wide-awake. This had never happened before, because Mom had explained to Alec and André that the bedroom door needed to stay closed at night, so I could not wander through the house and chew on something or have an accident. But, the boys had forgotten about the door! Now was my chance… free to explore the house with no one around! I was one lucky Beagle dog!

I slowly snuck out of my bed and crept to the open door. Looking back over my shoulder I saw Keekers looking at me with one eye opened. Yikes, I must have woken her! She hissed at me, "Don't do it". I paused, but the temptation was just too strong, so I headed downstairs. That pretty tree was calling to me, "Puppa-na-Wuppana come look at me"!

It was just as I remembered…sparkling with colored balls hanging all over it.   One by one I opened all of the boxes and bags that were tucked under the tree branches. I tasted and chewed on the boxes. I hid a few of my favorites in my secret hiding places to enjoy later. My tail wagged the whole time. This was one of the best nights ever! Suddenly, I heard Mom's voice … "Puppa-na-Wuppana! What have you done?! You have ruined all of the Christmas presents"!

Oh no, I must have been too noisy. Mom had woken up and she was very upset about what I had done!   I saw the tears on her cheeks and knew now this was no longer one of the best nights ever. "Puppa-na-Wuppana, all of those boxes and bags were not for you", she cried. "They were presents for the whole family and Santa brings your special Puppa-na-Santa toys on Christmas morning"! My head hung low and my eyes were sad. I had not heard of Santa and that I needed to wait for him. I guess not all Christmas Presents are for a Beagle dog to enjoy.

Keekers walked by and swiped at my face with her long, bushy tail. Looking over her shoulder she whispered, "Told you"!

"Mind your own business Keekers", I whispered right back. I did not like it when Keekers was right.

I went up to kiss and snuggle Mom. With my big, sad eyes, I looked at her so she would know how sorry I was. I had not known about Santa and Christmas morning and waiting for my own special Puppa-na-Santa presents. Now, I wait and open my very own Puppa-na-Santa presents with the rest of the family! Everyone is so much happier with that arrangement!

Puppa-na-Lost

The scariest day of my life was the day I got lost from my family. I was the saddest Beagle dog in the whole world! The day started off in the usual way, but on this particular day, my special and magical Beagle nose led me astray.

Each day, when Mom left for work and Alec and André went to school, my "Gramps" came to visit with me. I loved this time. Gramps would open the kennel door, rub my tummy and give me hugs. Then we would go outside and play for a little bit. Gramps gave me a treat every day and you know how this Beagle dog loves his treats.

It was a beautiful sunny day and Gramps was doing some yard work. I just did what I always did. I sniffed the great smells on the ground and looked for something to play with. Suddenly, I saw the most beautiful butterfly and I knew right away I wanted to play with that! I started to run after it but when I reached the end of my tie out, I could not go any further. So I just tugged and stretched a little and off came my collar! I was free! I ran and ran and ran to keep up with the butterfly. Oh my goodness, there were new smells everywhere and before I knew it, I had forgotten all about the butterfly and just followed all the delicious smells my magical nose was finding. This world was so big and exciting!

Suddenly, I realized that it was dark out and I was very thirsty and very tired and most importantly, I was very hungry. I looked around for Gramps. Oh no! Not only did I not see Gramps, this was not my yard either! Where was Gramps? Where was I?

Then I saw some children playing in a nearby yard. I ran up to them. Maybe they could help me find my house! The children giggled when they saw me and one of them ran into the house yelling, "Mom! Come and look! There is a lost dog in our yard"!

A lady came to the door, looked down at me and said, "What an adorable Beagle dog! Oh my, you have no collar. You kids are right! He must be lost. Bring him inside and we will try to find his family". I was scared, hungry and tired, so I was glad this family liked Beagle dogs. This lady gave me some yummy dinner and I soon fell asleep on a rug by her front door. This lady was nice, but I really just wanted my own Mom back.

The next morning, after a worried and sleepless night, I found out this lady was not as nice as I had first thought. Instead of taking me to my family, she dropped me off at a huge scary building with lots of barking and crying dogs. She told the man at the gate I was a lost dog. Oh no! I was at the home for lost dogs! I had heard scary stories about this place and I did not want to be here! Where was my family?

I was miserable. I missed my family and I could not sleep. The floors were very hard and there was so much noise! Dogs were barking and howling all night long! My goodness, I do not bark or howl. Mom says I am an extra special Beagle dog and calls me her "barkless" Beagle! Why did everyone there have to be so loud? All that barking and howling gave me a headache!

Suddenly, I heard my name, "Puppa-na-Wuppana"!! I looked up and there was my family! I was never so happy to be scooped into their waiting arms and covered with kisses.

That night, while we were snuggling in Mom's bed she told me how everyone had been so sad when they could not find me. They thought I might never come back to them. They had searched and searched and even put my picture all over the neighborhood in hopes someone had seen me. Gramps felt extra bad, as he was the one taking care of me when I tugged out of my collar. He called all the lost dog homes and told them all about me and that is how they finally found me.

Who would have thought this magical nose of mine was the cause of such sadness and tears! It usually only brought me joy. I vowed to be extra careful with its magical power as I never wanted to be lost from my family again!

Puppa-na-Doggies

I was so excited the day I found out I have other family too! They did not live with us in our house, but had a house of their own. Keekers told me they were my "doggie cousins"...whatever that means, and their names were Kingston and Kinlie. Keekers doesn't care for them as they bark all the time. We go to visit them quite often and sometimes I even get to have a sleepover! My "doggie cousins" live with Auntie Angie and Uncle Shay and they are long and skinny and very low to the ground. They also have so much more hair than I do! Kingston always greets me with his special howling bark! Kinlie is much shier, but I am sure that is because she secretly has a crush on me.

Their house always smells delicious! Uncle Shay makes food in the kitchen all day long. I have found it to be a little distracting, because I am trying to play with my cousins and my magical nose keeps tingling and leads me back into the kitchen. I can always count on finding lots of yummy things on the floor to eat! Sometimes I hear Mom call me "the cleaner" because the kitchen floor is very clean when I am nearby. I am sure being "the cleaner" is a special thing, because after all, I am a very special Beagle dog.

A visit with my cousins is always fun, but I am ready for a nap when I get back home. We play together so long and hard that sometimes I will sleep the whole next day! Even though I am tired, I am also a little sad. I already miss my "doggie cousins".

Puppa-na-Talian

Nana and Gramps live in the big house on the hill. I was only able to have one sleepover there. It did not go well, but that was really not my fault. I am sure you will agree with me once you hear the story. Mom dropped me off with my leash and some toys and told Nana and Gramps, "He is a Beagle dog, so he thinks he is always hungry, but only feed Puppa-na-Wuppana this much food, once a day, and only at dinner time". Mom also brought my "sleepover" pillow for me to sleep on at bedtime on Nana and Gramp's bedroom floor.

My dinnertime came and went and Nana gave me just the amount of food Mom had said. But then, as Nana was cooking dinner for her and Gramps, my magical nose sprang into action. Nana's kitchen smelled so wonderful. Everyone says she is "talian". I am sure "talian" means "lady that cooks great Beagle snacks"! I looked at her with my "hungry" face and batted my Beagle brown eyes at her (this works for me quite often) and Nana fell under my special spell. I had never eaten this "talian" before, and Nana was very generous with her grandpuppa, as most Nanas can be! I was so full and so happy!

The trouble came after we went to bed... tummy troubles to be exact. My tummy woke me up with a grumble and a rumble. I did not feel so well. I did not know how to wake up Nana and Gramps to tell them I needed to go outside for my "business" and I had quite a few accidents all over their bedroom floor.   It must have been a few too many, because I no longer get any sleepovers at Nana and Gramps house. I guess they do not care for accidents any more than Mom does.

Puppa-na-PUPS

Sometimes we go to Lori's house for a visit.
She is Mom's best friend and she loves dogs! I
have become great friends with her two dogs,
Lucky and Nala. Lucky is a lot bigger than I
am and black like Keekers. At first I was a little
nervous around her because she was so big, but I
soon found out she had a heart as big as she was!
Lucky always had to have a toy in her mouth and
her tail wagging when she ran to the door to say
hello to us! Her favorite game was to run up and
down the fence in Lori's backyard and bark at
people walking by. I soon found out it is best to
stay out of Lucky's way during this game as I am

much shorter and she didn't always see me running next to her!

Nala actually looks a lot like me and Mom says she is part Beagle dog. I am not sure which part that is, but I think it is her nose; because Nala has a sniffing nose almost as good as mine! She can be a little grumpier about sharing her toys and treats than Lucky, but as long as we have our noses to the ground and discover new smells, we get along just fine. Sometimes, though, our noses get us into a little trouble. Who knew you weren't supposed to dig holes in the yard trying to get bugs from the ground?

I love playing in Lori's backyard. It is big and fenced and I can just run…no leash or tie out! Lucky and Nala have a few less rules at their house too! They are allowed on the furniture! I get to nap on the couch or snuggle in the chair right alongside of them! Visits to Lori's house are so much fun!

Puppa-na-PW

When my family grew bigger, it was a very exciting time. I now had two sisters named Paige and Maggie and a Dad named Jon. Mom calls him Honey. Mom met Dad and they fell in love. What is love you might ask? I have no idea, but it made them smile and kiss a lot! Having more people around to snuggle and kiss me was the best part about this falling in love thing.

I will tell you something very funny. Dad would only pet and kiss me when no one else was home. He said it was our secret because the rest of the family thought that he was not much of a dog lover. Of course it was not long before I won him over. After all, I am a special Beagle dog. Who could resist me? He calls me PW and I love the secret special bond Dad and I share every day. He takes me with him on errands and buys me special Puppa-na-Snacks!

Since our family had gotten bigger, we moved to a bigger house. What a busy place! Alec, André, Paige and Maggie were coming and going all the time!   I heard Mom and Dad mutter "teenagers" under their breath several times a day.

Everyone loved our new house at first, except for me. There were quite a few new "Dad" rules about where I could and could not go in this big new house. This took a little time for me to get used to. All and all it was really not so bad.   I have two big beds…one in the back hallway and one in the kitchen. They were so comfortable and

Dad always put a toy and a treat in my beds for me. I could be around the family in the kitchen if I wanted or have some peace and quiet in the back hallway if I wanted that instead. Teenagers you know!

The best time was when Alec and André came home from school and I could go downstairs to their rooms and hang out!   No special new house rules down there!   I slept wherever I wanted! It was wonderful! My favorite, though, was crawling under the covers and snuggling in a bed all night long!

Puppa-na-Pink

My sister Paige loves the color pink. Her whole room was pink! She had a beautiful pink flamingo she kept on her bed.   Her boyfriend had given it to her and she loved to cuddle this pink flamingo all the time.

I too, felt a special bond with her pink flamingo and one day when she wasn't looking, I took it into my own bed to cuddle and kiss it.   I soon discovered, that was not such a good idea. Paige was very upset when she found me snuggling with her precious pink flamingo. She scowled and said, "Yuck…now my pink flamingo

has doggie drool all over it"! She stomped back
to her room and closed the door in my face.

I did not understand. Why was I now
locked out of a room that held so many pink
treasures I had not yet gotten to snuggle with?
That made me very sad. No one had ever
complained about my kisses before! The boys
always told me my kisses were something special.
Well, apparently not special enough to give to
Paige's pink flamingo.

Puppa-na-Puffs

My crazy magical nose again! It was always smelling stuff that I wanted to put in my tummy.

One time it was almost the end of me. I was downstairs where the boys had been watching the TV and found a large plastic bottle with some orange puffy things at the bottom. They smelled delicious. I looked around. The boys were gone! I quickly stuck my magical nose inside the bottle opening but I could not quite reach the puffy things at the bottom. I pushed really hard… swoosh…I got all the way to the bottom and started eating. I had never before tasted orange puffy things. There are certainly none of these in my treat cupboard. They were so good that I ate all of them and even licked the bottom of the bottle clean. The trouble came when I tried to get my head back out of the bottle. I couldn't! The bottle was stuck on tight! Soon I realized there was not much air for me to breathe in the bottle either!

I needed to find Mom right away! I ran up the stairs to the living room, banging the bottle against the walls the whole way up. I heard Mom say, "Who is making all that noise"? When she saw me with the bottle stuck on my head, she screamed, "Maggie, come quick! Puppa has his head stuck in a bottle and he cannot breathe. I need help"! Mom sounded scared and that made me scared too!

Maggie came running to help. She held me

very still while Mom got a scissors and carefully cut the edge of the bottle away from my neck! With a whoosh it came off and I could breathe again! Mom and Maggie hugged and kissed me. "Puppa-na-Wuppana. Please don't ever scare us like that again", mom cried!

I had given my family a real scare and not only that, I had to suffer through getting a bath because the fur all over my head was completely orange from the puffy things! I will tell you a secret, though, those orange puffy treats were worth it!

Puppa-na-Chocolate

My magical nose gets me into a lot of trouble. This time it was because of chocolate. I guess Beagle dogs are not supposed to have it. I am not sure why but I wish it wasn't true, because it is very delicious.

One evening when my family was out, my nose sniffed the air and found a new and exciting smell! I followed it to a bowl sitting high up on the counter top. I had to think fast. Keekers jumps high on counters. Why couldn't I? A jump and a paw swipe and the bowl crashed to the floor. Out spilled delicious smelling little brown

balls. I tasted one…mmmmm…then another and another. Before I knew it, I had eaten the entire bowl!

When Mom and Dad came home they found me lying on the kitchen floor. I usually run right up to them to kiss them hello, but not this time. I had a terrible tummy ache. I looked at them with very sad eyes. Mom and Dad looked at me and then at the empty bowl and quickly figured out what had happened. "Puppa-na-Wuppana"! Mom cried, "You ate the entire bowl of chocolate candies. Beagle dogs cannot have chocolate. You must go to the veterinarian. You could die!"

They scooped me up and ran out to the car. Mom had tears in her eyes and even Dad looked a little scared. They laid me in the back seat and we headed down the road. We had not gotten very far when my tummy began heaving and all that delicious chocolate came right back up and all over the floor of the car. Dad did not look happy. He wanted to go home and start cleaning the car, but Mom said we should go to the veterinarian anyway just to be safe. Dad rolled his eyes, but we drove to the doctor as Mom wanted, because that is the way things work at our house.

I was feeling better and did not think we needed to go. It is not my favorite place. After Mom explained to the nurse what had happened, she gave me some medicine and soon my tummy was heaving again... and again... and again... until there was not any chocolate left in my tummy.

After we got back home, I went right to my bed and lay down. I was so tired. I sure hoped I did not have any dreams about chocolate balls and doctor visits. How can something that tastes so good when eaten, be so horrible coming back up? Chocolate is not worth going to the doctor!

Puppa-na-Posh

My family sometimes goes away for a few days. They call it a vacation and they tell me there are certain vacations that dogs cannot go on with their family. I did not like the sound of that. The first time this happened, I was very sad and a little worried.

Mom and Dad just patted my head and said, "Don't be sad, Puppa-na-Wuppana, you are going to the Doggie Hotel". They explained it was a special place where doggies could be on vacation at the same time their families were on vacation. Mom assured me I would have fun there and make new friends. I was not so sure. How could being away from my family be fun? I didn't need any new friends! I was very nervous. Especially when Mom let the word "kennel" slip. What! She knows how I feel about a kennel!

When we got there, I was very happy to discover that Mom was right! I really should have known this though, because as Dad tells the family quite often, "Mom is the Queen and she is always right".

It was an incredible place full of other dogs whose families couldn't take them on vacation either! I met so many new friends and played and played with them all day long! It was all very exciting, but just a little too loud for my liking. My new friends really seemed to enjoy themselves and barked very loudly and very often at all the other dogs vacationing at the Doggie Hotel. I

just wagged my tail at everyone, because as you remember, I am different than most Beagle dogs. I am Mom's very special "barkless" Beagle.

Once I got a little too excited after Dad brought me to the Doggie Hotel. I think seeing all of my friends and playing with them was just a little too much excitement for my tummy. I started to feel a little funny and then suddenly all of my breakfast came right back up!

The Doggie Hotel veterinarian was worried, so they called Dad to make sure it was okay to take me to the emergency pet hospital for some tests.

Dad was on the golf course and not very happy about the interruption, as he knew exactly how delicate my tummy can be, but he also knew Mom would want to be sure, so he told them to go ahead and take me for the tests. When they called him back to say I was fine, Dad sighed and said, "Yes, I thought that might be the case. He has a sensitive stomach". Mom gets very worried about those kinds of things, but I could have told everyone it was just from all the excitement at the Doggie Hotel.

I cannot wait to go back. I sure hope they want me to come back to stay with them again too. After all, the mess was not really all that big of a problem to clean up.

Puppa-na-Ouch

Sometimes my big floppy Beagle ears give me trouble. I never know when it is coming, but all of a sudden they sting and itch and I just shake and shake my head trying to get the itch out. I guess this happens quite often with Beagle dogs.

Thankfully Mom always notices right away. She runs to the cupboard for my special drops. I try to hide when I see this, because even though I know they make me feel better, getting those drops in my ears is not fun at all. Mom kisses my nose and says, "Puppa-na-Wuppana, you know I have to do this to make your ears better. I will try to be as gentle as I can". Then she grips my head tightly in her arm so I stay still and holds my ear back. I close my eyes tight and then in go the drops! It tickles a lot! I really shake my head when she is all done, but before long I feel so much better and the itch is gone! Mom was right again—as usual. As we all should know by now!

Puppa-na-Sneak-a-Snack

My brothers, Alec and André, know how much I love snacks and so they are my allies when it comes to making sure I get plenty of them! The three of us have a secret system so Mom and Dad do not find out just how many snacks I am actually getting!

One night the boys and I were watching a movie. The doorbell rang and a hot and delicious pizza showed up for the boys to have for dinner. I immediately lost interest in the movie and kept a watchful eye on that pizza. The smell drove my magical Beagle nose crazy!   Alec and André ran upstairs to get some soda to have with their pizza. I waited only a moment and then I helped myself to three big pieces. Delicious! Pizza tasted just like Nana's "talian"!

The boys were not happy with me when they got back downstairs and saw what I had done. "Mom", they both cried, "Puppa-na-Wuppana snuck three pieces of our pizza"! Mom just sighed and said, "Oh that magical Beagle nose of yours Puppa. It got you into trouble again"!

Mom does give me dog treats now and then as she doesn't know how many "secret" treats I get.   I won't ever say no to a treat, but they do not compare to "talian".

Recently, I figured out how to open my treat cupboard door with my paw.   I was very excited

about this, but helping myself to my Puppa-na-Treats did not last long. Mom found all of the empty wrappers lying on the floor! You see, I have not yet figured out how to open the trash bin lid to throw away the evidence! Now my Puppa-na-Treats are kept in a different cupboard way up high where I can't reach them. My Mom is so smart.

Puppa-na-Special

When the weather is nice I go on lots of walks through our neighborhood with Mom and Dad. We meet all sorts of people on our walks. Some of them have their dogs with them too. It is so much fun to sniff and wag tails with the neighbor dogs! Everyone we meet says, "What a cute Beagle dog"! Then they always ask the same question, "What is his name"? Mom tells them my name with pride…"It is Puppa-na-Wuppana"!

It is funny to see people tilt their head to one side and try to say my name. They generally do not get it right the first time. It is a tongue twister. They must practice though, because the

next time they see me, the children squeal with
delight and clap their hands and say, "There is that
Puppa-na-Wuppana dog! He is the cutest Beagle
dog with the most special name"!

They are right of course. My name is
Puppa-na-Wuppana! I have a magical nose and I
am very special.

The Real
Puppa-na-Wuppana

About the Authors:

Cindy Koebele

The Puppa book series has been a long time vision of mine. Living with the "real-life" Puppa has provided my family with countless hours of entertainment, joy and exasperation. I wanted to share this with the world. I asked my best friend, Lori Weaver, to collaborate with me on this project and the exciting Puppa-na-wuppana series was launched. I also own and operate a successful title insurance company in the St. Paul/ Minneapolis Twin Cities metro area and providing "over the top" service to my customers is a priority to me in everything I do. I live in the cute town of Mahtomedi, Minnesota with my loving and supportive husband Jon. I have two wonderful sons, Alec and André, two beautiful stepdaughters, Paige and Maggie and of course a lovable Beagle with a Magical Nose.

Lori Weaver

I am a self-employed title closer and share my home in Vadnais Heights, MN with two of my five wonderful children and our adorable rescue dogs, Nala, and Marscaponie. Lucky, Puppa's friend from chapter 9, has crossed the rainbow bridge. Dog rescue is very near and dear to my heart and I volunteer for a wonderful local organization, SafeHands Rescue. Cindy Koebele and I have been best friends for over 15 years. She is "my person". I was honored when she asked me to collaborate with her in making her long time vision of "Puppa" into a reality. I hope everyone falls in love with Puppa as much as we have!

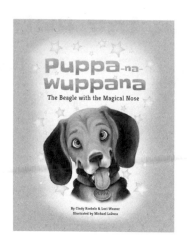

Puppa-na-wuppana

The Beagle with the Magical Nose

By Cindy Koebele & Lori Weaver
Illustrated by Michael LaDuca

Check out the Puppa-na-Wuppana picture book at puppabooks.com!

The entertaining story of "Puppa-na-wuppana, the Beagle with the Magical Nose" is based on the real life antics of Cindy Koebele's very own beloved Beagle! The real life Puppa-na-wuppana, is always having new adventures, so watch for new books about this mischievous and loveable Beagle coming soon. Puppa-na-wuppana will delight children, adults and everyone who loves dogs!

Future Books

Puppa-na-Besties

Puppa-na-Keekers

Puppa-na-Santa

Puppa-na-Radio

Puppa-na-Cousins

Puppa-na-Vacation

Check out my site
puppabooks.com
and follow me on
social media!

Facebook.com/puppabooks

Twitter: @Puppanawuppan

Instagram: Puppanawuppana